ADVENTURES IN THE KINGDOM™

RESCUED FROM THE DRAGON

Written by Dian Layton.
Illustrations created by Al Berg.

Illustrations created by Al Berg.

Published by MercyPlace Ministries

MercyPlace is a licensed imprint of Destiny Image®, Inc.

Destiny Image® Publishers, Inc.
P.O. Box 310
Shippensburg, PA 17257-0310

ISBN 0-9677402-2-3

For Worldwide Distribution
Printed in the U.S.A.

This book and all other Destiny Image, Revival Press, MercyPlace, Fresh Bread, and Treasure House books are available at Christian bookstores and distributors worldwide.

For a U.S. bookstore nearest you, call **1-800-722-6774**.
For more information on foreign distributors, call **717-532-3040**.
Or reach us on the Internet: **http://www.reapernet.com**

CONTENTS

CHAPTER ONE

The laughter of children poured out from the castle walls and echoed throughout the Village of Peace and Harmony. Villagers looked up from their work and smiled. Their children loved spending time with the King. It used to be that those same children needed to be coaxed to go to the King's Celebration once a week, but now they ran up the Straight and Narrow Path to the castle every morning.

The children of Peace and Harmony were very interesting and unusual children. HopeSo, KnowSo, and Yes were always confident and out-going. Giggles, Gladness and Glee loved to have fun. Dawdle and Slow talked and walked together very slowly. Doodle and Do loved to discuss which one of them would get to DO something. And Seeker, the boy who used to lead his friends to the CARNALville of Selfishness, was now seeking to know more about the King.

Today there was another kind of seeking going on. The children had spent the morning sliding down the shining castle hallways and playing in the underground waterfall, but now they were in the castle's Royal Courtyard. Seeker and his friends were playing a game of hide and seek, and the King was "It."

The King had been playing the game with a lot of energy, when he suddenly looked very, very sad. He went and sat down on a bench, and the children gathered around him. The expression on his face made the children feel worried.

"Are you all right, King?" Seeker asked. "What's the matter?"

The King smiled a sad smile and answered, "Thank you for your concern...but I'm fine..."

"D-d-don't you l-l-like playing hide and seek, King?" Dawdle asked.

"A-a-aren't you having fun, King?" Slow asked, patting the King's shoulder.

An even greater sadness filled the King's expression. "Sometimes," he said quietly, "seeking for people who are hiding is not very much fun."

The children were puzzled. "What DO you mean?" asked Doodle. "You can always find us, King! You just pretend not to know where we are!"

The King smiled. "I can find you because you want me to. But...there are some people who don't want me to find them." When he said that the King leaned back in the

2

bench and his sadness was so great that the children felt like crying.

Seeker watched the King, wondering. There was something familiar about the King's sadness...something very familiar....The other children were startled when suddenly Seeker cried out, "Now I remember! Hey, King! You looked sad that other day, too!"

The King appeared puzzled. "What other day, Seeker?"

"You know—that other day!" said Seeker, "That day at the Celebration! The day you winked at me during the banquet!"

"Oh..." replied the King, "You mean like this?" He leaned forward and winked. Seeker and the other children laughed.

"Uh-huh!" answered Seeker. "Well, that day you were looking at the third banquet table—you know, the empty one, and you were looking so sad. Why were you sad that day, King?"

"And why DO you look so sad today, King?" Do asked sincerely.

The King looked at the eager young faces around him and said, "Do you REALLY want to know? The reason I am sad means very much to me...And I can't tell you about it unless you REALLY want to know."

"We want to know, King!" the children said with all their hearts. "We REALLY want to know!"

"All right, then, I'll show you!" The King stood to his feet and pointed at one of the castle towers. "Come—we have to climb the Lookout Tower."

3

CHAPTER TWO

Seeker and his friends followed the King through the wooden door of Lookout Tower and down a wide hallway where the royal building supplies were kept. Giggles, Gladness, and Glee playfully danced with the paint cans and mops and hoes before climbing up the tower's winding stone staircase.

Lookout Tower takes some people quite a long time to climb, but the Kingdom children quickly reached the top. "Wow!" exclaimed Giggles. "You can see for miles up here!"

Gladness pointed, "There's Peace and Harmony!"

"Look!" shouted Glee, "There's our house!"

"And look over there!" Seeker said.

"There's that old selfish CARNALville. It sure looks small from up here!"

Everyone agreed. After a few moments, while the other children kept talking and pointing excitedly, Dawdle and Slow remembered why they had climbed the tower. They turned to the King, "D-d-does this t-t-tower make you s-s-sad, King?"

"No," the King answered, "the tower doesn't make me sad—it's what you can see from the tower. Look—way over there! Tell me what you see."

The children looked off into the distance, and they saw a dark, gloomy village. And as they looked harder, they could see it more and more clearly. (Seeing more clearly is what happens when the King shows you something from Lookout Tower.) The village had walls around it but the walls were broken down. There was garbage everywhere and junk was piled up almost as high as the roofs of the buildings. The houses looked as though they hadn't been cleaned or painted for a very long time. Weeds were growing instead of flowers, the trees had bare branches without leaves, and the lawns looked like they had never seen a lawnmower.

The children looked even more closely...trying to see if anyone actually lived in the village. Then Seeker pointed and yelled, "Look! There at the gate—a dragon! A great big dragon!"

"Oh, yuck!" cried Giggles. "It's picking its nose!"

"That is so disgusting!" Yes said, standing closer to the King.

"That is so gross!" Glee said.

6

"That is so nauseating," KnowSo stated, holding his stomach.

"That," the King said sadly, "is...the Dragon Greed."

The tone of his voice made the children turn to him soberly. "The Dragon.... Greed. Is that what's been making you feel sad, King?"

The King nodded. "Very, very sad. The Dragon Greed is the ruler of the Village Greed. He breathes thoughts into the people's minds continually—thoughts of getting, and having, and never sharing!" The King sighed a great sigh and continued. "I love those people so much! I want them to come to the Celebration, and eat at my banquet! I want to bring them out of Greed and into my Kingdom!"

Seeker nodded, understanding now. "Hide and seek...you want to FIND those people."

Do moved closer to the King and asked earnestly, "Then why don't you DO it, King?"

"Yeah, King, rescue them just like you rescued our families from the Dragon Fear!" Seeker turned to explain to his friends. "It happened a long time ago. My mom told me all about it."

"Rescue them from Greed just like how you rescued us from the CARNALville!" HopeSo said, and the other children nodded, remembering.

Just then the King quickly reached forward and pulled Yes away from the edge of the Tower. She had been leaning too far forward and was about to lose her balance. "Yes!" she cried in relief. "Those people need to be rescued! Whew!"

7

The King nodded. "I want to rescue them. I want to set them free from the dragon's power; I want to FIND them...but they don't REALLY want me to! They like being greedy..."

"They like it?" echoed the children in surprise.

The King nodded sadly. "Yes, they like being greedy; and they have heard that if they come into my Kingdom, I would take everything away from them, and I wouldn't give them anything."

The children were shocked. "You wouldn't do that, King!" said Seeker. "You don't love to get—you love to give!"

"You know that, Seeker, and I know that..."

"But they don't know that!" the children shook their heads together.

"What I need," the King continued, "is someone to go and tell them the truth about me!"

8

The children leaned thoughtfully along the tower ledge. "I wonder who could go tell them about the King?"

"Hmm…" said the King, looking at all of the children, "I wonder?"

Suddenly, Giggles said, "I have an idea, King! Send a messenger!"

The King shook his head. "I've tried that."

The children looked at each other, shrugged their shoulders, and then leaned thoughtfully along the tower ledge again. "He's tried that."

"Hey!" Gladness said eagerly, "How 'bout having a BIG party and inviting them to come!"

The King shook his head again, "They're not interested."

"They're not interested," the children echoed sadly, shrugged their shoulders, and again leaned thoughtfully on the tower ledge.

"There's got to be something you could DO, King!" Doodle said.

"I KNOW, King!" KnowSo spoke up excitedly. "How about an army!?"

"YES! An army!" Yes cried.

All of the children began to imagine a great army of fine Kingdom soldiers marching toward Greed and conquering the fierce dragon.

Do slipped his hand into the King's and asked hopefully, "DO you HAVE an army, King?"

The King smiled a mysterious smile, "Yes…a little one."

Doodle felt discouraged, "It's not very big, eh?"

"Hmm…" the King continued to smile mysteriously, "I think it's big enough."

"W-w-where is your army, K-K-King?" Dawdle and Slow asked, "C-c-can we see it?"

"It's not far away! In fact, it is very, very close," said the King. "Close your eyes real tight… and I'll show it to you!"

The King gently took hold of each child by the shoulders and turned them slowly. "Okay, you stand here. And I'll put you right there. Keep your eyes shut, now! Okay, and you over here." The King lined the children up in a circle so they were facing each other. "There! Now open your eyes and see my army!"

"What?!" The children were absolutely shocked. They pointed and cried, "Him?! Her?! Us?! We are your army, King? Really?!"

Seeker and his friends were very quiet for a moment; then they all said together at exactly the same time, "Uh-oh."

The King laughed a deep, happy laugh. "Why are you so surprised? I have chosen you, and you are my army. You will go to the Village Greed and tell the people there the truth about me! You will be my powerful Kingdom soldiers!"

The children were very quiet for another moment; then again they all said together at exactly the same time, "Uh-oh."

"Come on," said the King. "Let's go back down to the courtyard."

The children quietly followed the King back down the winding stone steps of the Lookout Tower. No one spoke because each child was thinking about what the King had showed them.

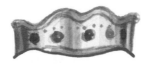

CHAPTER THREE

When they reached the castle courtyard, the children sat down. Finally, after several moments, Seeker broke the silence and said what all of the children had been thinking, "You know, King, I don't think we can do this. We're just kids!"

"We want to tell those people who live in Greed the truth about you, King," Doodle said, "we REALLY DO; but they wouldn't listen to us. We're just kids!"

"Just kids?!" the King repeated. "Listen, in my army, the size of a person has nothing to do with whether or not they are a good soldier." The children looked at him doubtfully, and the King continued, "In fact, here in my Kingdom, someone who appears to be small can actually become the most powerful!"

13

The children looked at the King, trying to believe him. Then Do sadly shook his head, "Sorry, King. We just can't DO it!"

"I just KNOW they wouldn't listen to us, King!" KnowSo said.

The King laughed again. "It will take some time, and it will take some work...but you *can* do it! They will listen to you!"

"B-b-but...wh-wh-what about the d-d-dragon?" cried Dawdle and Slow."

"Yeah!" agreed the children. "What about the dragon?!"

Yes moved closer to the King. "Yes," she said, "What about the dragon? It's a very big dragon, King."

"The dragon appears to be big," nodded the King, motioning for the children to come closer, "but he can only be as big as you let him be. I will teach you a song to sing to the dragon Greed, and the song will make him lose his strength! Listen carefully now, this is the song:

> *We don't love to get, we love to give!*
> *We don't love to get, we love to give!*
> *Serving the King has made us sing,*
> *And loving the King means everything!*
> *We don't love to get, we love to give!"*

The King repeated the song several times and the children learned it quickly. As they sang along, courage filled their hearts, and no dragon seemed big enough to ever be able to stop them. When the children finished singing, they bowed and curtsied, and the King applauded. "You must go to the Village Greed in a spirit of generosity!" he said.

14

The children looked at the King, puzzled. "Wh-wh-what's g-g-generosity mean?" asked Dawdle and Slow.

"It means LOVING to give!" the King answered. "Give your time, give your service, give, give, GIVE!

The children were puzzled. "But King, what can we give? We're just kids!"

The King acted surprised. "Just kids?! " The children smiled, embarrassed that they had so quickly forgotten that size didn't matter in the King's army. The King laughed and picked up a rake that was leaning against one of the courtyard walls. "Alright, soldiers, here are the kinds of tools you need to defeat the Dragon Greed! You will overcome greed with—giving!"

Giggles, Gladness and Glee caught on right away. They ran through the door of Lookout Tower and came back with hoes and brooms, buckets and cans of paint.

"We can take hoes to hoe their gardens; brooms to sweep their floors!" Glee announced brightly.

"Soap to wash their windows, and paint to paint their doors!" Giggles laughed at the rhyme.

"I will mop the floors until they shine like new!" said Gladness, laughing.

"Mowing lawns is something that I like to DO!" said Doodle.

"I HOPE I can take Mom's homemade bread!"

"Uh, uh..." KnowSo scrambled to find a rhyme, then smiled. "I KNOW she wants the people FED!"

15

The other children laughed and slapped KnowSo on the back. Then they stopped laughing when they realized the King was watching them with one of his mysterious smiles.

"Good," nodded the King, "Very good. You shall overcome greed with giving! And every kind thing that you do, no matter how small it might seem, will be powerful against the dragon." The King motioned to the children to come close to him.

"When you go to the Village Greed, I want you to tell them the truth about me. I want you to take a most important message to them...a most important message." As he said those words, the King became sad again. It was like a great weight settled upon his heart. The children gathered around him quietly, and the King spoke to them with such sadness that they felt as though they would cry with him.

Yes climbed up onto his knee. "What is your message, King? What do you want us to tell them?"

The King looked around at the children's faces and whispered, "Tell them...that I love them."

Tell them there's a King who loves them.
Tell them there's a King who cares!
Tell them there's a King...Who loves them—
A King who gives and shares!
I want to give to them new life in my Kingdom;
I want to give them my joy, and my peace.
I will fill their hearts with happiness, and laughter
As they really get to know Me.

"We'll tell them, King," the children whispered back. "We'll tell them."

Then the King spoke to them in his most kingly voice, "Alright, you are my army! Giggles, Gladness, and Glee," the three children turned quickly when the King called their names, "I want you especially to remember the song about giving. Be ready to cheer on the troops!'

Giggles, Gladness, and Glee stood like soldiers and saluted as they sang, "We don't love to get, we love to give, sir!"

"Doodle and Do!" When the King called their names, Doodle and Do stood at attention. "DO your best!"

"Yes sir! We'll DO it, sir!"

"HopeSo, KnowSo and Yes—Do not be afraid; you will be fine soldiers!"

I HOPE so, sir!"

"I KNOW so, sir!"

"YES, yes of course we will, sir!"

"Seeker!" Seeker saluted and stood ready to hear the King's words. "You shall lead the troops!"

"Yes, sir!"

"It's going to take work, and it's going to take discipline!" the King said as he walked up and down the line of soldiers. "Now, go home, get a good night's sleep, and report for duty at sunrise!"

"Yes, sir!"

Then the King saluted, winked, and went into the castle.

The children continued to stand at attention. Do asked the question they were all wondering. "DO you think we're really the King's army?"

"I HOPE so!"

"I KNOW so!"

YES, yes of course we are!"

Seeker took a step forward in front of the line and shouted, "Report for duty at sunrise! On with the adventure!" And the children of the Kingdom marched out from the castle courtyard, down the Straight and Narrow Path, and back to their homes in Peace and Harmony. They had a lot of work to do before the next morning.

CHAPTER FOUR

Early the next morning, near the forests of Laws Forgotten, the crow of a grouchy rooster filled the air. The dragon Greed stretched and groaned and stood to his feet in front of his village gate. With a loud belch of breath that smelled like rotten eggs, the dragon began to sing, as he did every morning, to an imaginary audience:

I am the Dragon, the Dragon Greed!
I rule this town—it is named after ME!
I breathe lovely thoughts to my people —
Dreams and dark ambitions;
I fill their heads with greediness,
And lots of selfish wishes.

The dragon stood, picking his nose while thoughtfully thinking about the people who lived in Greed. *They are under my control—I'm the one who feeds them! Yet, the yearning in their souls never, never leaves them!* Just then, the people of Greed came to the gate to report to the dragon. He laughed a very wicked laugh and then proceeded to go over his list of greedy people.

"First, there's the Mayor—Mayor Miser the Mad! His wife is ungrateful, snobbish, she's Mad! Their off-spring make my greedy heart glad! Their names are: Stingy, Persnickety, and Just Bad!"

"Then there's my friend, the Baker Moocha More-eh, and his wife, Mucha More-eh and their daughter, Megga More-eh!"

"A young and old maid—two favorites of mine—dreaming and scheming and wasting their time! Auntie Ambition and Fanciful tell stories; and their stories are all...lies!"

"Mr. and Mrs. Smudge Yukerty, the town cleaning crew! Dark, Dingy and Dirty help make things look like...uh...new!"

Alright then, everyone, let's sing the Old Town Song, shall we?"

Every morning the Dragon Greed led his people in a song. The villagers were proud of the song and sang it with great enthusiasm.

We've— gathered up riches and wealth
and things we're not about to part with!
Greedily gathered and grabbed at things;
We've been so wonderfully selfish!

Our village has a name to uphold;
A rep—utation have we;

For miles around our fame is renowned;
We're known as the people Greed
(Hee-hee-hee-hee-hee!)

While the villagers sang their song, Dark, Dingy, and Dirty went throughout the crowd, taking things that weren't theirs. Smudge Yukerty had trained his children to steal. Today, Smudge's children had managed to steal Mayor Miser the Mad's gold watch and Just Mad's favorite pearl necklace.

The people of Greed were all very greedy, but in a variety of ways. Smudge and his family were greedy about having things that weren't theirs to have. Mayor Miser the Mad and his wife, Just Mad, were greedy for fame and power. They loved being the most important people in the village and they felt as though everyone else should serve them. Stingy, Persnickety and Just Bad got every single thing they asked their parents for, but when they got those things, they were only happy for about five minutes. Then they wanted something else.

Baker Moocha More-eh, and his wife, Mucha More-eh and their daughter, Megga More-eh, were greedy for food. But no matter how much they ate, they never felt full inside. Auntie Ambition and Fanciful spent hours dreaming and scheming and wasting their time. They made up endless stories of their travels and achievements, but none of their stories were true. They were greedy for

attention and liked to wear clothing and makeup that made people look at them.

The people of the Village Greed lived a terrible life of arguing, fighting, stealing, and always wanting more. And no one, especially the dragon, was expecting anything to ever change. And no one, especially the dragon, knew that at that very moment, an army was approaching the village.

CHAPTER FIVE

Yes, an army was approaching the village; an army of children. They were carrying hoes, rakes, brooms, mops, cans of paint, and boxes filled with good things to give and share; and they were marching on a path the King had made through the forests north of the World Beyond the Kingdom.

"Look—there's the CARNALville!" pointed Gladness. "I'm sure GLAD we don't go there any-more!"

"Just keep marching," Seeker warned. "Don't stop and don't even look at the CARNALville. We don't want to meet up with any dragon-clowns today!"

The others agreed and kept marching steadily toward Greed. It was mid-morning when they arrived at the outskirts of the village. Swarms of flies buzzed around the village walls. Bent and old looking trees without leaves were trying to grow along the path, together with weeds and tall brown grasses. The stench was incredible. The smell of rotten eggs swirled around the children. "Ugh!" Glee cried, holding her nose. "Where is that terrible smell coming from?"

"Next time, let's bring some air freshener!" Giggles said, coughing.

"And bug spray!" Glee said, trying to wave away some flies.

"Shhh!" Seeker pointed with an excited whisper."Look! THAT'S where the smell is coming from!"

"Dragon," the children were horrified. "The Dragon Greed."

"L-l-ooks even b-b-bigger close up...d-d-doesn't he?" stammered Dawdle and Slow.

Seeker put a warning finger to his lips, "Shh!"

Do peeked out from behind Seeker's back. "DO you think he's sleeping?"

"Well, there's only one way to find out!" whispered Doodle. "Go ahead, Do!"

"Me?!" whispered Do loudly. "No way! You DO it, Doodle!"

Doodle pushed his brother forward, "You can DO it, Do!"

Do stepped back and pushed his brother forward, "C'mon, Doodle—DO it!"

Seeker firmly stepped in front of them. "*I'll* do it! You all wait here! It looks like that gate is the only entrance to the village; I'll try to sneak around the dragon…"

The children called after him in anxious whispers, "Be careful, Seeker!"

Seeker moved bravely and carefully toward the dragon. Closer and closer, until he was almost close enough to touch the great beast. Seeker held his nose and tried to keep from getting sick. The dragon's breath was terrible and he smelled as though he had never, ever brushed his teeth; and never, ever taken a bath. Seeker pinched his nose tightly and began to step toward the entrance gate of the village. But suddenly…!

…The dragon stood up with a loud and vicious ROAR!

His size was even greater than before, and he towered above Seeker, whose legs were shaking violently. The dragon shouted, and his voice rumbled throughout the countryside. The rats and slimy crawling things scurried for cover. Even the flies buzzed away, fearfully trying to find a hiding place. "Who DARES to approach

Greed—unannounced! Uninvited!" the dragon shouted, his terrible breath rushing at Seeker, and his words dripping with disgusting green slobber. "Speak up, you, or I'll turn you into a heap of smoldering ashes!"

Seeker wiped drips of disgusting slobber from his arm and frantically called to his friends, "Wh-what was the song?! What was the song we're supposed to sing to the dragon?!"

Giggles, Gladness and Glee gulped. They remembered the song, but what good would it do against this terrible creature? Then the dragon reached an ugly clawed hand toward Seeker, and Seeker called out again, "Hurry! What was the SONG?"

Giggles, Gladness and Glee tried to call, but they were so afraid, that the song just came out of their lips like a little whisper, "We don't love to get...we love to give."

Instantly, the dragon winced in pain and turned his attention to Giggles, Gladness, and Glee. "I beg your pardon," he sneered, "WHAT did you say?"

Giggles, Gladness and Glee gulped in fear and whispered again, "We don't love to get...we love to give."

The dragon winced again and put his clawed hands over his ears. "Get away from here. Go away with your feeble little tune!"

Giggles, Gladness and Glee repeated the words of the song and the other children joined in, gradually singing louder and more confidently as they watched what the song did to the dragon. "Go away, you bad and nasty children!" The dragon growled at the children as he stood protectively in front of the village gate. "Go away! I hate your song! I hate your song!" But the children just sang more loudly:

31

"We don't love to get, we love to give!
We don't love to get, we love to give!
'Cause serving the King has made us sing!
And loving the King means everything!
We don't love to get, we love to give!"

"Serving the King has made you sing?" The dragon Greed whined, cried, and howled in a fit of rage. "Don't mention him around here! Bad and nasty King! Go away you bad and nasty children! Go away!"

"Sing again, louder this time," Seeker called.

The dragon roared in anger, held his ears, and shook his head back and forth in agony. He tried to shut out the song by grabbing a nearby trash can and pulling it over his head, but the children just sang louder and moved forward. The closer the children came, the more agony the dragon was in, and he seemed to get smaller. "Look!" cried Seeker. "He's shrinking! Sing louder, everyone! Sing louder!"

Sure enough, the dragon was shrinking, and the song had pushed him back so the entrance gate to Greed was no longer blocked. The children saw what was happening. "Hurry!" they cried. "Go through the gate!" Still singing with all their strength, the army of children ran past the miserable dragon and into the Village Greed.

Glee turned and pointed at the dragon as she ran though the gate, "We're not bad and nasty children! YOU are a very bad and very nasty dragon! And the people who live here are about to know the TRUTH about the King!"

"No! No!!" the dragon cried desperately. "You can't go in there! It's my village!!! They belong to me! Don't tell them about the King!! No!! No!!" He fell in front of the gate sobbing loudly. " No!!! Please don't tell them about the King!"

But much to the dragon's anger, the children from the Kingdom of Joy and Peace were already in the Village Greed. And they were already at work—singing, sharing, giving, and telling the people the truth about the King who loved them!!!

CHAPTER SIX

Seeker and his friends kept visiting the Village Greed every day. The children began each morning by spending time with the King, and then off they marched, singing their songs. Gradually the Dragon Greed had become weaker and weaker, until he could no longer guard the door; and when he saw the Kingdom children, all he could do was moan a pitiful moan.

The people of Greed were concerned, very concerned. One day all of the villagers were called to attend a Town Council Meeting—all of the people except the Greed children, that is; they weren't invited. (But if anyone had been watching closely, they might have noticed Dark, Dingy and Dirty; Stingy, Persnickety and Just Bad; and the baker's daughter,

Megga, sneaking underneath the tablecloth, where no one could see them!)

Everyone chattered in concerned, anxious voices as they took their places at the Town Council table.

Mayor Miser the Mad pounded the table to get everyone's attention. He cleared his throat and spoke in his most dramatic voice, "This emergency meeting was called tonight to decide what we're going to do. These kids, they keep coming—they're giving and loving—we just don't know quite what they're up to!"

Just Mad stood to her feet. "I'm in a state of frustration, and I'm losing my patience!" she wailed. "And it's all because of these kids!"

(Beneath the table, the mayor's son, Just Bad, was in trouble. He was allergic to flour and he was hiding right beside Baker Moocha More-eh. Each time the baker moved, clouds of flour settled under the table. Just Bad was struggling not to sneeze.

Auntie Ambition stood to speak, fanning herself dramatically, "Their singing and bringing have set our heads spinning—we can't understand these kids!"

Smudge Yukerty spoke with deep concern, "The dragon's power is weakening—it seems always he's sleeping, and hardly guarding the door..."

"I've noticed he's not eating, that's sure not in keeping," said the baker slowly. "And I've hardly heard him roar!"

At that very moment a low and painful moan was heard. (Everyone thought it was the dragon, but it was actually Just Bad, still trying his best not to sneeze.)

36

"There, now, you heard that!" the baker said. "The dragon's sick and that's a fact!"

Mrs. Yukerty stood to her feet, crying, "The streets have been clean-swept; the houses been up-kept even the doors have been painted! All my windows are shining, my floors aren't so grimy, and there aren't any weeds in my garden!" She sat back down, sobbing and wailing.

Smudge put his arm around his wife and then said, "These children! Why do they come here, day after day? Why do they serve us—and why don't they want any pay?!"

The villagers looked at each other. "Why don't they want any pay?"

They were shaking their heads in confusion and concern, when suddenly the villagers heard a loud sneeze! "What was that?" cried Mayor Miser the Mad.

"It wasn't the dragon, that's for sure," The Baker Moocha More-eh said slowly.

"Then who was it?!" demanded Auntie Ambition nervously.

"It was me!" Just Bad announced. He crawled out from under the tablecloth, wiping his eyes. The Greed children all crawled out from their hiding places one by one...and the villagers were amazed.

"What are you doing here?!" yelled Just Mad.

"What have you got to say for yourselves?" asked the mayor.

"I need a tissue!" declared Just Bad.

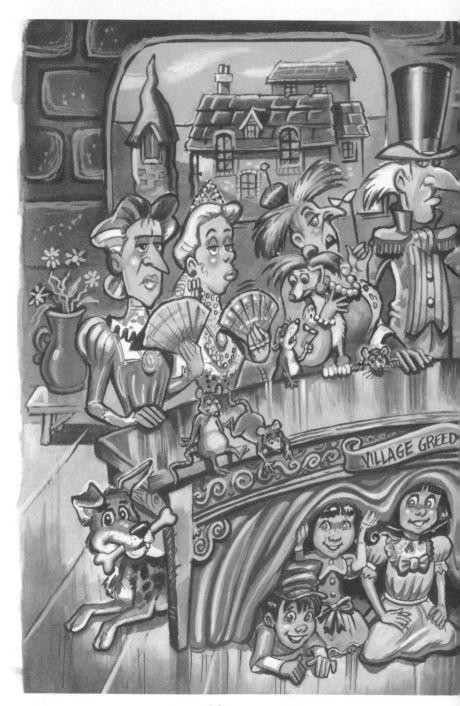

His mother handed him a tissue. "Now answer my question! What are you doing here?"

Just Bad blew his nose. "We LIKE the kids who have been coming to our village!"

Stingy stood beside her brother and said, "These children have brought us laughter; these children have brought us joy!"

"These children have taught us manners!" Persnickety said with a bow.

"We've even been sharing our toys!" Just Bad said proudly.

"Sharing your toys?!" The villagers echoed in dismay. Sharing anything was absolutely unheard of in the Village Greed. Mayor Miser the Mad was terribly embarrassed by his children. His wife was, of course, Just Mad. Fanciful and Ambition fanned themselves dramatically and then fainted.

Dark, Dingy, and Dirty stepped forward and quietly set a string of pearls and a gold watch on the table in front of the mayor and his wife. The children had stolen these earlier during the Old Town Song. The mayor gasped in surprise, "My gold watch!"

"My pearls!"

"My goodness!" Smudge exclaimed at the unusual behavior of his three children.

"And they've taught us some beautiful songs!" Stingy declared. "They say there's a King who loves us!"

40

The villagers gasped in shock at such a statement. Ambition and Fanciful had been just getting back up off the floor, but at this, they fainted once again. The baker's daughter stood beside her mother. "What's love, Mother?"

"What's love?" Mucha More-eh echoed. "What's love? Why, I suppose it's the very thing I've been wanting MORE of all these years!" and she reached out to hug her little girl.

"They say there's a King who cares," Stingy continued.

"What do YOU care about, Daddy?" Just Bad asked the mayor, but the mayor couldn't answer. Instead, he pulled his three children close and began to cry.

"The King sounds wonderful!" Persnickety said. "We must leave our Village of Greed!

The villagers looked at their children in dismay. "Leave Greed?!" echoed the mayor. "But our village has a name to uphold! A reputation have we! For miles around...our fame is renowned! We're known...as the People...Greed."

Instead of their usual pride in that fact, the villagers suddenly felt embarrassed. "We're known...as the People...Greed..." they repeated softly.

"Please!" said the children to their parents. "Let's leave Greed!"

For a few moments there was silence, then Smudge Yukerty said, "Perhaps an investigation would be in order to find out the reason why these children have crossed our borders! Why? Why? Why?"

41

The Greed villagers nodded their agreement, "Why do they come here, day after day? Why do they serve us? Why don't they want any pay?"

Mayor Miser the Mad pounded the table with great authority. He cleared his throat and spoke with his most dramatic voice. "Meeting adjoined! We will meet the children..."

At that very moment, there was another kind of pounding...actually it was a knocking. The villagers looked at each other in surprise. Just Mad went to open the door. There in the entrance stood the children from the Kingdom.

CHAPTER SEVEN

"Hello!" Seeker said. "We're sorry to bother you! We just wanted to let you know we're leaving now. We'll see you all again tomorrow." Seeker and his friends turned to go, but the mayor stopped them.

"Wait! Don't go!" The Kingdom children turned back questioningly. The mayor cleared his throat and spoke with his most dramatic voice, "Uh...we of the Village Greed have a question to ask you..."

The villagers nodded and stepped forward together. "Why do you come here day after day? Why do you serve us? Why don't you want any pay, no way? Why don't you want any pay?!"

Seeker and his friends smiled. "We come because the King sent us," Seeker answered. "He really loves you."

The villagers leaned forward with interest. "He does?!"

"Yes!" said Seeker. "He REALLY loves you!"

The mayor cleared his throat again. "Well, in the past, we have heard rumors about this King—how he makes his people give up everything—he doesn't let them have anything!"

"Oh no!" Seeker cried. "The King's not like that at all, he's wonderful!!"

"Like you kids?" asked Just Bad.

Seeker was embarrassed by the little boy's compliment. "No, the King is much, much better than us!"

"Yes, he is always giving, and giving!" Yes nodded.

HopeSo and KnowSo stepped forward and spoke to the mayor. "The King sent us here with a very important message for you!"

The children sang the King's message, and the people listened closely. The villagers knew that they needed to change...and here was the answer, the amazing answer. There was a King—a King who loved them and wanted to give them a new life!

There is a King who loves you;
There is a King who cares
There is a King who loves you –
A King who gives and shares.
He wants to give you new life in his Kingdom;
He wants to give you his joy and his peace.
He will fill your hearts with happiness and laughter
When you really get to know him!

During the song, the people of Greed began to cry—softly at first, and then in loud wails. Just Mad and Mrs. Yukerty, who had been enemies for years, held each other and sobbed. "I'm so sorry for all the things we took that belonged to you!" Mrs. Yukerty cried.

"And I'm so sorry I didn't think to share them with you!" cried Just Mad. "I've spent so much time being mad, just mad!" Smudge passed out tissues, giving several handfuls to the mayor, who seemed to be crying even more loudly than everyone else.

The baker and his wife hugged Fanciful and Auntie Ambition. "We've been so busy trying to fill the emptiness inside that we never took time to care for other people!" Moocha More-eh said, crying.

Auntie Ambition and Fanciful responded tearfully, "And we told lies to you about how full and happy we were! But we weren't full; we've been empty, so empty!"

When the children finished singing, the mayor blew his nose a final time and cleared his throat, "Well, I believe I speak for all of us (the villagers nodded their agreement); we're tired of being greedy! It seems we've always had what we thought we wanted, but never got what we REALLY wanted…if you see what I mean…"

"I've always dreamed of being happy," cried Fanciful, "but I've never *been happy*."

"I've wasted so many years," wept Auntie Ambition, "dreaming and scheming."

Mrs. Yukerty stepped forward. "But we didn't really know there was a better way…until you children came here and told us!"

"Until you children came here and showed us!" Smudge Yukerty exclaimed. "Now we know WHY you've come here every day—it's because of HIM!!"

"Because of HIM!" Seeker nodded excitedly. "Because he LOVES you. He wants you to have a brand new life in his Kingdom! He wants you to get to KNOW him."

The mayor cleared his throat loudly. "Well, I believe I speak for all of us (the villagers nodded their agreement); we want to...we need to...get to know the King."

"Hooray! Hooray!" The Kingdom children cheered, then remembered something very important. "Oh, just a minute! Do you really want to know the King?"

"Uh -huh!" the villagers responded.

The children shook their heads and folded their arms firmly. "Uh-uh!! Do you REALLY want to know the King?

"Yes!" the villagers responded with great enthusiasm. "We REALLY want to know the King!"

"Then you SHALL know the King!"

To the absolute surprise of everyone, the King himself stepped out from a place near the village where he had been waiting to be found.

"The KING!" The Kingdom children crowded around to greet the King, while the people of Greed watched with shy amazement. It was really true. There truly was a King! And here, all those years, they had believed a lie. They had believed a lot of lies.

The villagers rubbed their eyes and looked again at the King, when suddenly, from beside the gate came a terrible ROAR!

The Dragon Greed summoned his last remaining strength and rushed toward the crowd. The people screamed and immediately fell back. The villagers held their children closely and trembled with fear.

The dragon was definitely smaller than he had been. His strength had slowly been destroyed by the children's giving, and he was now so small that his clothing sagged around his frail body. But the dragon's anger had not grown smaller; it had grown very, very big. He rushed toward the King with hatred streaming from his face. His breath came in disgusting green smelly gasps. "They are under my control!" he screamed in a slobbering rage. "I'm the one who feeds them!"

"They belong to you no more!" said the King with calm authority. "This day I've come to free them!"

The King folded his arms and stood tall and strong in all of his majestic royal power. Then the King lifted his voice and began to sing. It was an incredible song. The King's words and music sent the walls of the Village Greed tumbling to the ground. The dragon writhed in pain. He circled the King, roaring and whining and crying...and shrinking even smaller than he already was! And still the King sang...

Loving to give,
not loving to get;
Singing, and sharing,
Greed to forget.
Selfless, not selfish,
Hearts that are pure—
Lives filled with rejoicing;
paths that are sure.
Loving to give,
not loving to get;
Singing and sharing —
Greed to FORGET!

48

Then the King laughed. He laughed and laughed and laughed. Then he laughed some more, until, with one final angry roar, the dragon disappeared. (It had returned to its wicked master in the deep dark place beneath the trap door of the CARNALville of Selfishness. From there, sadly, it would likely be sent to work at other Greed villages beyond the mountains.)

After a few unbelieving moments, the villagers whispered in amazement, "It's gone! The dragon is gone!" The village children jumped up and down and cried, "Hooray for the King! Hooray for the King!"

The King looked at his army of children, leaned forward, and winked. "Fine work, everyone! A little bit of giving can overcome a lot of greed!" the children smiled back at him happily.

"Well, King," Seeker said, "I guess we'd better introduce you to everyone!"

"Yes, Seeker," nodded the King. "I want to give each person a new name!"

Do took hold of the King's hand and lead him over to the mayor, who was nervously bowing his head. "This is the mayor!" Do said.

The mayor continued to bow his head. He spoke softly, embarrassed at who they had been. "Yes, uh, Your Majesty, I'm Mayor Miser the Mad. My wife here, she's Just Mad, and our three children are Stingy, Persnickety, and Just Bad."

The King reached out to welcome the mayor and his family into his Kingdom. "From now on you shall be Mayor Giving and Glad! Your wife shall be Just Glad, and your children shall be Sharing, Fairness, and...and you," the King said as he knelt down to look Just Bad in the eye, "you shall be called, Just Good! Do you think that you can live up to that name, son?"

Just Good smiled and said, "Yes sir. If you REALLY help me!"

"I will help you!" the King said, standing to his feet.

Yes took his hand next and introduced the baker's family. "This is the Baker Moocha More-eh, and his wife, Mucha More-eh and their daughter, Megga More-eh!"

The baker was holding his family and blowing his nose loudly. "Excuse me, sir, it's just that we've always wanted MORE, but nothing ever filled up the emptiness..."

"Until now!" the baker's daughter, Megga, cried out and threw her arms around the King.

The King picked the little girl up in his great arms and twirled her around. His laughter filled the air and swept through the streets of the village, removing even more traces of what had always been. The King's laughter burst into the hearts of the people, and for the first time in their lives, they felt happy and full.

The King touched the baker and his family, saying, "You are the Baker BountiFULL; your wife is FULLfillment, and your daughter is JoyFULL."

Giggles lead the King over to Auntie Ambition and Fanciful, who were fanning themselves nervously. "You will find the happiness you have dreamed of in my Kingdom," the King declared, "and your names will be Hope and Destiny!" The ladies smiled radiantly at the King and curtsied.

"This is Smudge Yukerty," Gladness announced.

"Hello, Your Majesty," Smudge bowed low. "Meet my wife, Mrs. Yukerty, and our three children, Dark, Dingy and Dirty." Smudge reached out to shake the King's hand, then suddenly realized how dirty he felt...how dirty he *was*. He tried to wipe his hands off, but they just looked worse. He stood, very embarrassed, in front of the King. Then to Smudge's complete amazement, the King reached out and hugged him close!

"From now on," the King said with a sparkle in his eyes, "You shall be Smudge Cleaner!" And instantly, Smudge and his family were sparkling clean!

"Oh!" cried Smudge. "I'm Smudge Cleaner now!"

"Mrs. Cleaner," the King smiled, kissing her hand, "and your children are Bright, Neat, and Tidy!" Mrs. Cleaner giggled shyly and hugged her family close.

"And now," the King said to the villagers, "I will tell you about your new home in my Kingdom!"

"Where is our new home, King?" asked the village children.

"It is called the Village of Generosity!" The King smiled a mysterious smile. "It's not far away; no, in fact, it is very, very close!"

The King began to tell the people all about their new home. And he told them in a song. The villagers hugged each other and wept and danced as the King sang.

In the Village of Generosity—
You will live in the
Kingdom of Joy and Peace;

I have prepared a place especially for you
And you, and you, and you!
I will take away your selfish hearts;
I will give you lots of loving thoughts,
All your anxious worries—they will cease
I give you peace...
I will pour My love inside of you;
Clean hearts you'll have inside of you;
You won't love to get —
You'll love to give!

Something wonderful happened as the villagers hugged each other and wept and danced and sang. The Village Greed melted away, and in its' place, the Village of Generosity sparkled in the sunlight. Certain parts of the old village remained. Certain parts like the carefully weeded flowerbeds, the freshly mowed lawns, and the newly painted doors. The King had used every gift that the children of the Kingdom had given—every helpful and kind thing they had done—to help build a new home for the villagers.

"Thank you, King! Thank you, children! Thank you for rescuing us from the dragon!" the villagers cried.

The villagers turned toward Generosity and made excited happy comments as they entered the gate. "Oh, it's wonderful!" "It's even better than wonderful—it's magnificent!" "It's more than anything I could ever have imagined!" "It's absolutely beautiful!" "It's absolutely home."

Seeker and his friends watched the people of Generosity go into their new homes. Then the children walked with the King back to Peace and Harmony. Giggles took one of the King's hands and asked, "Anybody want to play another game of hide and seek when we get back to the castle?" Everyone laughed.

The next week at the King's Celebration, the third banqueting table was filled with the happy, laughing people from the Village of Generosity. The King looked over at Seeker and his friends, leaned forward, and winked. The children quickly got up from their places at the banquet tables and ran up to the throne.

"Look, King!" Seeker said happily, "your banquet is full!"

The King didn't answer. The children looked at each other in surprise. The King still didn't speak; he just smiled one of his most mysterious smiles. Something about the way the King's eyes twinkled, and something about his mysterious smile, made Seeker and his friends realize that their adventures in his Kingdom had only just begun.

THINK ABOUT
THE STORY

The best part about this story is that it is TRUE!

There truly is a Kingdom of Joy and Peace, and there truly is a King.

The sad part of the story is that there is also a dragon. One of his names is Greed.

Every person has to choose—whether or not they will live in the Kingdom, or if they will live a selfish life of greed.

Where will you live?

TALK TO THE KING

"King Jesus, I don't want to live my life in the Village Greed; always wanting more, but never feeling full and happy inside.

I want to live in your Kingdom like Seeker and his friends.

I want to be part of your army. Help me to destroy the power of greed by giving.

I want my life to be an adventure!"

Don't be overcome by evil; overcome evil

with GOOD! (Clap-clap!)

(From the Great Book – Romans 12:21
Hugga-Wugga ™ Paraphrase)

Land of Laws Forgotten

VILLAGE GREED

CARNALVILLE

Valley of Lost Dreams

World Beyond
the Kingdom

Island of Despair

ROYAL HARBOR

Talking Tree Forest

Peace

Harmony

The Kingdom of Joy and Peace

N
E   W
S

Adventures in the Kingdom™
by Dian Layton

━ SEEKER'S GREAT ADVENTURE

Seeker and his friends leave the *CARNAL*ville of Selfishness and begin the great adventure of really knowing the King!

━ RESCUED FROM THE DRAGON

The King needs an army to conquer a very disgusting dragon and rescue the people who live in the Village of Greed.

━ THE WHITE TOWER

The children of the Kingdom explore the pages of an ancient golden book and step through a most remarkable doorway — into a brand new kind of adventure!

━ IN SEARCH OF WANDERER

Come aboard the sailing ship, "The Adventurer," and find out how Seeker learns to fight dragons through the window of the Secret Place.

━ THE DREAMER

Moira, Seeker's older sister, leaves the Kingdom and disappears into the Valley of Lost Dreams. Can Seeker rescue his sister before it's too late?

━ ARMOR OF LIGHT

In the World Beyond the Kingdom, Seeker must use the King's weapons to fight the dragons Bitterness and Anger to save the life of one young boy.

━ CARRIERS OF THE KINGDOM

Seeker and his friends discover that the Kingdom is within them! In the Land of Laws Forgotten they meet with Opposition, and the children battle against some very nasty dragons who do not want the people to remember...

Available at your local Christian bookstore.

For more information and sample chapters, visit www.reapernet.com